MW01043752

OWEN'S

TERRARIUM

Pam,
To wheels of
brie & classic
horrors

Julie
Hiner

THE TERROR INFLICTED BY OWEN'S TERRARIUM

"Owen's Terrarium is a delicious treat for any reader who loves the dark and twisted. A disturbed protagonist meets his match in this quick and spine-tingling read."
JJ Reichenbach, Secretly a Demon and Author of the Nix Series

"A story superbly written and intense, I had to stop to take a breath and then delve right back in. An amazing read!"
Bri the Scared

"I love that Julie has created a fascinating character, Owen, a meticulous perfectionist that thinks so descriptively. I almost see, feel, and taste while reading. What does he miss? The attention to detail is astounding."
Jennifer Palmer – Founder/Podcast Host OnlineforAuthors.org

Owen's Terrarium © 2021 Julie Hiner

All rights reserved. No part of this publication
may be reproduced, stored in a retrieval system,
or transmitted, in any form or in any means –
by electronic, mechanical, photocopying,
recording or otherwise –
without prior written permission. All events,
locations and characters are either fictional or
used in a fictional way, as products of the
author's imagination.

First Printing 2021

Publisher: Julie Hiner
KillersAndDemons.com

Editing by: Taija Morgan
Bio Photo by: Aune Photo
Cover Design: Julie Hiner

ISBN: 978-0-9958243-9-3

First Edition

To Jack.

The one driven by sickness,

and longing

for the innards of his human shell to flourish,

as he followed a painful curve,

and built a house.

GOODBYE BUTTERFLY

April 12, 1980

Owen narrowed his eyes, staring down at the butterfly pinned to a square of white oak. Its wings, the colour of an ocean, spread out around its body. The sickness swirled through his veins, searing him with pokers of sharp pain. The butterfly twitched. The only way to end his suffering was to end the butterfly's.

He raised his hood, tucking his dark locks behind his ears. A shiver crept down his spine. There wasn't enough meat on his wiry frame to fend off the chill of the basement.

He pushed on the flat top of the pin. The butterfly fluttered its wings in a desperate attempt to escape its fate. The silver weapon slid deeper into its body. Black-purple oozed with a painful slowness from the tiny hole piercing its flesh.

The ocean wings fluttered wildly, slapping against the white oak, pieces tearing from the delicate paper-like flying contraptions. Owen pushed harder. The pin pierced through the other side of the body. As the wings slowed to a twitch, Owen's shoulders relaxed. Minimal damage had been done by the butterfly's frantic flapping. The butterfly wasn't going anywhere. It twitched again, and this time the tremor caused a convulsion to ripple through its entire insect body.

With a final push, the pin hit the white oak. The thick inner fluid of the arthropod trickled down both sides of the cylindrical body, staining the wood. Not for long. Owen knew from experience that white oak didn't stain permanently, and that with a dab of his homemade concoction on a cloth, he'd be able to clean up the backdrop of the butterfly's forever home.

It was best. To be able to secure the insect to its permanent afterlife dwelling while it still breathed. To be able to watch it twitch slowly to its end, the last few breaths dissipating from its body as it finally lay still.

Owen licked his lips. He picked up a pair of tweezers and clamped them to the bottom end of the butterfly's tubular physique. With deliberate precision, he guided the pin, still piercing the creature, up toward the butterfly's head, causing a gush of innards to escape in a thin line of black-purple sludge.

Ocean wings twitched. Once. Twice. The body convulsed three times. The butterfly lay still, accepting its fate.

Owen's shoulders relaxed. He removed the pin, myrtle hemolymph oozing down the thin, silver weapon. He removed the tweezers, purple-black chunks of insect flesh sticking to the open prongs. He wiped the pin, placed it on the wooden table, then wiped the tweezers, placing them next to the pin.

Placing his hands in his lap, he stared at his work. Nothing moved. The silence in the room deepened, as if the entire space had taken a deep breath and exhaled slowly into a meditative state.

The dim lightbulb hanging from the centre of the wooden rafters flickered, then went out.

Owen stared into the dark basement, the shapes of forgotten sheet-covered furniture loomed around the perimeter of the musty space. It was the only place Owen could find any peace. He was the oldest of the dozen children Agnes—Mrs. Harden—had collected. She was like the old lady in the weather-beaten house who collected cats. Only, Agnes collected children. Unwanted orphans abandoned by their mothers, or thrown into the evil core of the earth by tragic events that took away the few parents who actually wanted their spawn. Agnes loved lonely orphans. Owen had been the last one added to her collection. At sixteen years old, he'd been shocked at the news that he'd be leaving the wet basement of the dark convent.

The bulb flickered back on, casting long shadows from the furniture over the cold, concrete floor.

Owen stared at the butterfly's body. Dead. The long, bulbous black cylinder bleeding out, even after the twitching had stopped. Owen's mind spun. Hot blood pumped through his veins, boiling his skin. Sweat sprouted over his forehead, trickling down his face.

Its body morphed, the dark tube contorting into a naked, small figure. A human figure.

Owen blinked several times. The butterfly face turned up toward him, two dark bulbs peering, questioning. Pale pink flesh pushed through the black skin casing, ripping a fissure, splitting the face between the round, black eyes.

Fleshy salmon cheeks burst through the insect skin. The beady insect eyes fell away as the casing that housed the insect body split open. Bright-blue eyes stared back at him—innocent, fresh, unharmed by the evil of the world.

The young boy's flesh was moist with the fluids that kept it safe inside its mother's womb. An innocent young being birthed into a world of evil. Its cheeks were wet with mucus, the bright-blue eyes exploring his, seeking him.

Owen stared at the spitting image of himself. His own eyes, his own body, the day he was born. The day he was pure. The day he was clean from the filth of the world. Owen's bottom lip quivered. A tear escaped from the corner of his eye, trickling down his sweat-soaked cheek, mixing with his stinky sweat.

The slimy pink lips of the newborn child moved, releasing a tiny mewl.

Owen watched the infant lips as they released coo after coo. The soft sound slithered into the pits of his ears, soothing the flesh that had been burned by the evil words of a woman who, instead of loving him, had hated him. The bright-blue eyes sparkled under the fluttering blinks of the newborn's delicate eyelids. The baby cooed again, the fragile sounds wrapping soothing hands over Owen's hardened ears.

The hot sweat pouring over Owen's face, his body, sticking his shirt to his back, cooled to a cold, running river, soaking him in an ice bath. He shivered.

Owen shivered. His lips trembled.

A thump jolted Owen from his mind-contorting hallucination. The door at the top of the wooden staircase burst open. Light streamed down into the dark space, bringing the dust, must, and dinginess of Owen's makeshift workshop to life.

"Owen," Agnes screeched in her bone-rattling voice. "Owen, get up here. I need help with dinner."

But I'm almost finished. He bit his bottom lip, surpassing the urge to 'talk back', as Agnes labelled any response from any of her collectible orphans that contradicted her orders.

"Owen," Agnes screeched. "Did you hear me?"

Owen forced out a compliant response, lacing it with sweetness, "Yes, ma'am."

The door slammed shut. Darkness cloaked his workshop again. He breathed a sigh of relief. He would not ascend that staircase until his project was complete. He needed to sterilize the forever home of the butterfly corpse, and secure the glass casing. He would not risk any undue exposure to the beautifully manicured carcass he had pinned to the white oak. No way.

Owen focused on the butterfly. He concentrated on his well-practised cleaning script. He ignored the aromas of cheap meat thrown into a gloppy stew seeping from the kitchen upstairs. He blocked out the stomps and thumps from the kitchen above and the sounds of wailing children.

For now, it was just him and his newest prize.

His body relaxed. A warmth rushed through him, from the tip of his crown down to his core.

He scanned his cleaning toolkit, selected the right brush and the most potent cleaner, then went to work sterilizing and perfecting the forever home of the dead butterfly.

He hummed to himself, mentally scanning the collection hanging in a basement closet behind a forgotten couch. Where would he hang his new trophy? Would he nestle his new piece between the salamander and the lady bug? Or between the garter snake and the mouse? Or, was it special enough to mount next to the Praying Mantis?

He shook his head. *No, don't be silly, Owen.* The Praying Mantis was the trophy of all trophies. The day he had captured and mounted the magnificent creature…well…it had been a special day. A very special day, indeed.

Owen smiled wide, turning his attention back to the ocean-winged butterfly and his meticulous cleaning routine. There were five steps to the procedure. There were always five steps to all of his procedures. Five was the best number. There was something soothing about it. It calmed him. It made sense.

He picked up his bottle of homemade cleaner. Thanks to Agnes' need to keep her home free of the filth that her collection of children constantly left in their wake, she kept a healthy supply of all-purpose stain remover, all-surface heavy-duty cleaner, and dish-washing detergent in her basement closet at all times. Owen had discovered that the three mixed together made a powerful concoction perfect for removing stains and smell.

He sprayed his carefully chosen brush with the potent mix, mentally ticking off the first step on the checklist blinking in his brain, and went to work on the white-oak home of the deceased butterfly.

FILM AFICIONADO
April 13, 1994

A chill quivered through the musty air. Owen pulled his grey wool sweater off the back of the wooden chair and slid his arms into each sleeve. He was thin. Too thin, perhaps, to be working in this basement where the draft chilled his bones at least once per shift. The air system in the old building was inconsistent and unreliable. The temperature was unpredictable as a result. And those musty drafts swept through the dark basement on a regular basis, taking a wave of dust mites and bunnies along with it.

Owen had found the old sweater discarded in the basement when he belonged to Mrs. Harden's collection of children. He'd never seen another like it, with its wooden buttons and vintage pattern. The thick wool wove into an airtight sequence, keeping the draft out. He picked up a ceramic mug perched on the desk, steaming with a fresh pour of coffee, and took a long sip. The warm liquid soothed his insides. He was ready to work on the next reel.

The Elm Movie House was located in an old building. A few years back, there'd been a great dispute over the future of the movie house, since it looked ready to topple over at the slightest nudge. However, the brick building was none other than the *Royal Theatre,* part of the town of Macleod, Alberta, since 1903. Originally built as a theatre for burlesque and first-run films, it passed through many hands. Miss Vickie Estelle ran the joint for several years, where her ladies serviced the patrons in the most gentlemanly of manners. When Miss Vickie's business fell through, old George Caboose took over and ran the town's only distillery until the first wave of the prohibition hit in the early 1920s.

The building had sat vacant for several years after George and his drinkers were kicked out. A couple attempts were made to restore the theatre back to a place of entertainment, but it wasn't until Wilfred Thomas swooped in, in 1970, that it was properly resurrected into the finest entertainment establishment the town had ever seen—the *Elm Movie House.*

Each night at the Elm Movie House had a theme. Fridays were horror nights, Owen's favourite. He loved watching the crude monsters of make-believe feast upon the flesh of unsuspecting victims. Several evenings a week—Monday, Wednesday, and Friday, to be exact—Owen ascended from his regular station in the depths of the basement to the top floor, more of an attic, really, to run the film.

Since he'd been such a stellar employee for so long, he'd earned the spot of Friday Night Fright, starting at nine o'clock sharp. He had an inkling that he was the only one who wanted the spot, really, but he chose to view it as something earned, more of a position of sorts, at the height of the week. He supposed the other employees would rather be on dates or with family. He had nowhere better to be. Nowhere.

So, there he would perch in the cozy attic, the penthouse suite of the Elm Movie House, and run two horror flicks, back to back. One of them of his own choosing, since he had proven to Wilfred that he could select the most horrific delights and attract a slew of teenagers, flooding the seats.

The house was always full, so Wilfred was happy. Owen turned an eye to the occasional clanking of a bottle, or the rare raucous outburst that followed the consumption of such liquids that would be found in such a bottle. Thus, the teenagers were delighted and never missed a Friday Fright Night. Yes, Owen loved his Friday nights.

Owen pulled a fresh pair of white cotton gloves from the box on the corner of the wood desk where he sat, and slid one over each hand. He pulled the next box of reels his way and selected one of the circular, silver tins. He still marvelled at how perfectly matched his obsessive-compulsive traits were for this meticulous job that required the utmost attention to detail.

He set the tin onto the desk. He inspected the torn label, the black writing faded almost to nothing. *The Night of Dreadful Doris*. Well, he'd never heard of this one. What a treat.

He took the lid off and lifted the reel out of the tin. He positioned it, with the utmost care, onto the split reel in the centre of the desk. He slid a lightbox from the corner of the desk over to the positioned reel. Scanning a row of carefully placed silver tools, sterilized and laid out on a sheet of plastic, he chose one long, tweezer-like arms, and latched on to the first frame of film.

With a soft tug, he used the tweezers to pull the film, turning the reel. He fed the first frame into the lightbox, secured it, then snapped a switch, bathing the frame in bright light. The picture came to life. A woman, old and haggard like a witch, stared back at him, her beady black eyes bulging from her sickly green face, her hair wild and tangled, spilling over her face. *Hmmm. Dreadful Doris, perhaps.*

Owen inspected the frame, every square inch of it. No blemishes presented themselves. Satisfied, he readied the second frame for a close inspection.

Frame by frame, Owen inspected the entire reel of *The Night of Dreadful Doris,* ensuring every single particle of every single frame was in impeccable shape. If anything were to be out of order, he would need to mark it and place the reel in the box labelled *damaged.* Lucky for Dreadful Doris, her entire reel was in perfect condition, earning her placement in the box tagged *good condition.* So it went, the afternoon in the dimly lit basement, unaware of the hot sun shining outside.

It was midway through the reel depicting *The House of Blood* that Owen's body seized and tension seeped through his veins. A bead of sweat sprouted high on his forehead, trickling its way down to the corner of his eye. His eye twitched. The droplet coasted down his cheek.

Owen stared at the frame of *The House of Blood,* depicting a horrible man with a deformed face, seething with anger, dripping in sweat, leaning over his terrified victim. The victim, a young woman with dark, luscious curls drenched in sweat and blood, screamed in terror.

Her perfect white teeth were exposed as she yelled in a pathetic attempt to free herself from her looming fate. A blemish in the highly flammable cellulose nitrate scratched across the woman's face, down her chin, and over her otherwise unblemished neck. The laceration seeped into the frame, creating a gouge of horrific extremes.

Owen grabbed a small plastic box labelled *blemish markers,* opened it, and laid out the materials required to mark the frame as inadequate, potentially casting the film to the box of the tarnished, perhaps forever.

His temperature had cooled to normal. He rolled his shoulders a couple times, refocused on the lightbox, and prepared to examine the next frame. Owen hoped there wouldn't be any more glitches in his day. He preferred a blemish-free, stress-free shift, where reels were declared perfect. If *The House of Blood* had no more than a handful of damaged frames, then it stood a chance of being repaired and played again.

About three quarters into the reel of *The House of Blood*, a door slammed, pulling him from his concentration.

"Owen," Wilfred's frail voice called through the dark basement, muffled by the shelves upon shelves of boxes of reels yet to be judged.

Owen looked up from his work, watching Wilfred weave through the dark rows of reels. Wilfred's shadow loomed from between two tall shelves, making him look much larger, and scarier, than he was. Wilfred's meagre frame materialized. The looming shadow cowered, back to its suitable stance.

"Yes?" Owen inquired.

"I need you to come upstairs." Wilfred ran his wrinkly hands through his thick silver-white hair. He raised his matching eyebrows.

"Upstairs?" Several beads trickled down the back of Owen's neck.

"Yes. Brandon called in sick. I need you to fill in." Wilfred's thin mouth pursed, making it look like he didn't have any lips.

Owen looked back at the reel. The sweat capsules trickled down his neck, bursting as they hit bristles, sticking out as if he were cold.

"Owen, it's only for an hour. I called Susie in, she's on her way."

Owen stared at the nearly finished reel. It seemed so abrupt to leave it now.

Wilfred placed his hand on Owen's shoulder.

Owen jumped.

Wilfred retracted his hand. "I know you like to be down here. I know how much you care about the films. Don't worry, it won't be long. You can finish what you started when Susie gets here. Or tomorrow. Your shift is almost over."

Owen swallowed hard, seeking the imitation of agreement that he'd forced into his memory bank of human emotions. He smiled. "Yes, of course. I was just...focused." He smiled wider.

"Thank you, Owen. You are always so helpful." Wilfred turned to retreat.

Owen contemplated the unfinished reel. It had already been deemed to be blemished, but only one frame. The final decision lingered in the air. He hated to leave it, partially done.

The last day at his last job flashed into his mind. The last time he hadn't *blended in*. He couldn't risk that happening now. He loved this place. They all believed he was *normal*. The dark basement was his refuge where he could obsess, reel after reel, frame after frame, undisturbed, unguided, playing out his tendencies, using his best traits, the only consequences being praise for a perfect job.

Owen stood, removed his wool sweater, placed it over the back of the wooden chair, and clicked off the lightbox. He would do what was required. He would do what he needed to do.

He picked up the ceramic mug, walked across the room to a counter and a sink, rinsed out the glass and left it to dry.

He turned toward the staircase leading to the upstairs, the main area of the film house. The place where the general public flooded through the doors, chattering and fluttering and causing such a commotion. The place where he would have to interact with any random person who walked up to the main door and requested to purchase a ticket.

Where did Brandon usually work? The ticket booth? That wouldn't be so bad. At least there, Owen would be caged off from the people pouring in by a thick pane of glass. He could disguise his discomfort behind the glass and the microphone used to clarify their requests. His shoulders relaxed.

He ascended three stairs. But what if Brandon usually worked at the concession stand? There was no glass pane there. Owen would be completely exposed. He would have to talk directly to every random person who walked up wanting buttered popcorn, sugary fountain drinks, and chocolate treats. His shoulders clenched. More sweat drizzled down his neck.

Again, the day he didn't fit in shot through his mind. Again, he concluded he had no choice but to fit in now. Make Wilfred believe he was a normal guy who could work behind a counter at a film house, serving the guests he loved to share his choice horror flicks with.

He took a deep breath, steadying his heart.

He ascended to the top of the stairs, halted, and stared at the door. His head spun. His ears rang. He felt like he was in the front row of a heavy metal concert, electric guitar vibrations violating him, stinging the pits of his eardrums, jolting down his insides to the trench of his stomach. Nausea lurched, threatening to project his poached eggs on brown toast all over the door, spilling onto the top stair.

Get it together, Owen. He willed his carefully prepared breakfast to settle. The bread had been toasted to excellence, crisp, brown, not a single burned crumb. The eggs had been poached flawlessly, cooked on the outside, warm all the way through, seeping yellow yolks over the brown toast upon a poke of a fork. The thought of perfection, prepared by him, calmed him. The eggs returned to the core of his stomach; the nausea backed off. His mind stopped. He stared hard at the door. Determination took over him in one fell swoop.

BUTTER, ON THE HOUSE

Owen turned the knob on the door and burst through the other side. He was assaulted by a barrage of bright daylight, plush red carpet, golden accessories, and the grand chandelier sparkling a million diamonds over the entire room. A wave of hot air, infused with buttered popcorn and body odour, clouded over him. He refused to allow the nausea to resurface. He narrowed his eyes, homing in on the counter across the room, and found his target—Wilfred.

OK, Wilfred. Let's put on a show, for you.

He walked across the plush red carpet over to where Wilfred stood, waving at him, in front of concession stand.

Owen let go of the next frame to process in *The House of Blood* floating through his mind. He left the familiar musty cold of the basement behind and embraced the mix of heat, sweat, deep-fried and sickly sweet violating the room, closing in on him. He imagined a barrier, like a large bubble, closing around him, forcing away all of the violating sensations bombarding him. He focused on Wilfred. Finding his own smile, he pasted it over his face and walked up to him.

"Owen, great. Just in time." Wilfred smiled, placing a hand on Owen's shoulder.

Owen grimaced.

Wilfred retracted his hand.

Owen re-pasted the smile on his face. "Yes. Here I am." He used his cheerful voice, the one he'd practised over and over in front of his mirror in his bedroom.

"Owen, this is Kelly, she's new." Wilfred gestured across the concession counter toward a teenaged girl with bright-blue eyes, an eager expression flooding her face. "Kelly, this is Owen, he's one of our long-time staff members. He's our film processing expert. He can help you behind the counter until Brandon's replacement gets here."

Kelly pranced up to the counter, her blonde ponytail swishing back and forth like the tail on a galloping horse. "Hi, Owen."

Owen provided the required response, "Hello, Kelly." The glue on his pasted-on smile dried. It was successfully in place for the next couple of hours.

Wilfred intruded, "Brandon was supposed to help Kelly learn the ropes." He looked at Owen. "I'm sure you'll do a great job until his replacement gets here."

"Oh, yes, you can count on that," Owen's cheery voice responded.

"Well, I'll leave you to it, then." Wilfred nodded, turned, and walked across the red carpet toward the manager's office tucked away in the corner at the front of the main entrance, where he could watch everything.

Owen walked to the end of the counter, popped up the makeshift employee entrance disguised as countertop, and slid through. Closing the employee door behind him with a click, he inspected the aprons piled onto two hooks, looking for the least disgusting one. Finding the only one that appeared not to have any smears of chocolate or butter, he hooked the strap across the back of his neck and tied the belt around his waist. He looked over to the cash register, watching Kelly help a customer with a ridiculous smile, her voice like the sound of birds in a forest. No one could really be that happy, could they?

He sighed, refocusing on the tight space he would share with Kelly for the next hour or two. He hoped it wasn't more than an hour. He really wanted to get back to *The House of Blood*. He shoved the thought away, walked over to the dual cash registers, and scanned the room. Mid-afternoon on a weekday. He thanked his lucky stars that this was a quiet time—only one movie was playing this afternoon, and it would be starting in half an hour. He could get through this.

Kelly tended to the lone customer. Owen turned to inspect the popcorn machines. One of them had just finished popping. He picked up a silver scoop and tossed the popcorn, ensuring an even distribution of the heat blasting from the bright light at the top of the glass case. He replaced the scoop into its holder, closed the front door of the popper and turned to the other popper. Only a scattering of half-popped kernels cluttered the bottom.

"Should we pop a fresh bunch?" the birds in the forest sang in his ears.

He turned to Kelly. Her smile took up most of her face. "Uh, no. We'll have plenty with the batch that just finished. There's only a single matinee on weekdays, and it starts in half an hour. Even if the theatre is half full, we'll still have too much."

"Wow. You know a lot about this place," Kelly chirped.

"Uh, yes. I've been working here for a long time, I guess." *I should be in the basement.*

"Well, maybe you could show me around some more, since we don't have any customers right now."

"That would be fine." *The House of Blood is only three-quarters finished.*

"Can you show me the coffee machine?"

"Yes." Owen walked over to the coffee machine.

He was halfway through explaining the process of grinding and brewing when a voice called over the counter. "Excuse me, please."

Owen turned, expecting some sloppy kid who'd convinced his mom to take him to a movie instead of going to school, or some pimply-faced teenager who'd skipped out of class, or, even worse yet, a couple teenagers with long hair and ballcaps turned backwards, thinking they were too cool for school. Instead, Owen faced a woman. A beautiful woman. He could have sworn he was looking at a porcelain doll. Her skin was like milk. Pale, yet creamy. Her hair fell softly over her shoulders, like milk chocolate, shining over her head, curling on the ends, landing on her shoulders over her pink jacket. Her lips, cherry red, were full and supple.

"Excuse me, please, is it too late to purchase some popcorn before the show starts?"

Owen looked at Kelly. "I'll get this. You finish the coffee, you're doing great." His smile had stayed in place.

He walked up to the counter. "No, of course not. What size would you like?" His insides swelled with foreign warmth and tingles. What was happening to him? The only thing even remotely familiar was the relief that washed over him when he played with his pets.

"Oh, well, I *should* get a small, but, well, what the heck, how about a medium?" Her full, red lips smiled, revealing perfect white teeth. Orange blossom wafted from her, seeping into his pores.

The warmth turned to full-on heat. The tingles intensified. "Will do." He turned to the popcorn maker, plucking a medium bag from the pile. Opening the front of the maker, he turned to the porcelain doll. "You're in luck. Fresh batch just finished." He smiled. This time, it wasn't pasted.

"Oh, how lovely," she chimed.

He filled the bag, then turned to her. "Would you like extra butter? On the house."

"Oh, well, I can't refuse that."

Owen turned back, placing the full bag underneath the butter pump, and topped it with several squirts of melted yellow. He was careful to move the bag as the butter came out, distributing it evenly over the popped kernels. He handed the bag to the woman and continued to smile without trying. "Anything else?"

"Is that girl brewing fresh coffee?"

Owen glanced at Kelly. It did appear she'd been successful. The pot had a couple cups in it. "Yes."

"I would love a cup. Medium, please." The orange blossom intensified.

Owen turned toward the bouncing blonde ponytail, pondering how it was possible that it was moving when she wasn't. Was she always this bubbly? "'Kelly, could you please pour a medium?"

"Sure!"

Owen turned to the cash register, focusing on the buttons. Conflict whirled through him. The tingling heat was foreign, new, exciting, yet terrifying. He was used to the same thing, over and over. He was used to what he knew. What he could control. He punched in a few buttons. "That will be $6.66." Owen looked up, risking what would happen as he found the eyes of the porcelain doll with his own.

"What a bargain." Orange blossom swirled; red lips moved.

"Your butter topping was on the house. First-time special."

Her perfect milky hand reached over and handed him a crisp, ten-dollar bill. "How did you know this was my first time here?"

Owen's cheeks blazed. "I work here a lot. I don't remember seeing you." *How would you see her from your basement home?* He handed her the correct change.

She turned her hand over, letting the change fall into her silky, pale palm. "I've walked by here many times, but never came in. I've always wanted to. I had a feeling about this place. The selection of films is quite eclectic."

Owen's smile hijacked his face again. "Yes, we do offer a top-notch collection here." He was getting used to the hot tingling searing through him. He kind of liked it. "Do you like horror movies?"

Her eyes sparkled. "I *love* horror movies. Especially the old ones. The classics."

Electricity pulsed through Owen. His mind buzzed. He could have sworn he was alone, at home, with his pets. He'd never felt this way around another person before. "We have a Friday Fright Night."

"That sounds intriguing." She popped a few kernels into her mouth.

"Every Friday." He laughed. "Thus, Friday Fright Night. Nine o'clock. Back-to-back features. One chosen by the film house. The other chosen by me."

Her right eyebrow raised in interest. "Oh? You're an expert."

"Well, at least an experienced viewer. I tend toward the classics."

Kelly popped up behind him, placing a steaming cup of coffee on the counter. "Here you go, freshly brewed." She stood close to Owen.

Owen cranked his neck, turning his face toward Kelly. "Thank you, Kelly."

Kelly stood still for a moment, then jerked. "Oh, yes, of course." She flittered off.

Sound boomed from the open doors of the single theatre in use for the afternoon. "Your film is starting," Owen stated.

"Thank you for the on-the-house butter." The woman picked up the coffee in one hand, the bag of popcorn in the other, and turned toward the theatre doors. A young man in film-house-employee attire had closed one door and was about to close the other.

Owen called out, "Hey, hold on."

The film house employee jerked, saw Owen waving, then held the door for the woman.

Just as she was about to enter the door—propped open by the employee's tattered sneaker—she turned and looked back at Owen. "See you on Friday night."

Owen's smile took over his entire face. He nodded and waved. The hot tingles heightened. As she disappeared through the door, they dissolved into a pulsing warmth.

PETUNIA AND BRITTANY

Owen turned the key, unlocking his townhouse, and shoved the door open with his elbow. The humid air hit his face, moistening his cheeks. Even though he'd sealed off the terrarium as much as possible, some of the humidity still seeped through the main floor. The walls were of inadequate quality to provide a one-hundred-percent-sealed enclosure. A complete makeover would be required—including ripping out and rebuilding the walls—to achieve the perfect state. Until he could finish his special project overhauling the basement, his exotic collection would have to be housed on the top floor. A minor inconvenience for the hours of pleasure he got from his special pets.

He closed the door with the heel of his shoe, then walked through the main entrance, setting a paper bag loaded with groceries on a long table lining the entrance hallway. The shiny black of the table top contrasted boldly with the dark-blue wallpaper. A large mirror—rectangular, with an ornate, charcoal border—hung over the centre of the table. He'd upped his game on the decor to the entranceway to match the rest of the rooms after the major overhaul he'd done when he'd moved in.

The townhouse was well organized. Everything had its place. The decor had a high-class flair. After slipping off his shoes, he walked to the kitchen, put the bag of groceries down, and fished out the wheel of triple-creme brie. He opened the stainless-steel fridge door. He smiled and exhaled a deep, calming breath. The sanitized shelves were organized perfectly. He placed the gourmet cheese in the appropriate spot, then walked down the hall to check on his precious pets. He'd been thinking of them all day.

He walked to the back of the kitchen, through a doorway, down a long hallway, and approached the terrarium. He unlatched the ring of keys hanging from his belt, found an ornately carved one, and slid it into the lock. It clicked as he turned it. As soon as he opened the door, the moist heat stuck to his face. His precious pets loved to be warm and wet.

He walked along the rows of glass tanks lined up along all three walls of the room without a door, their panes scrubbed and polished to a shine. The wall with the sealed door displayed a set of controls for monitoring the conditions of the room and the lighting. Pausing at each glass home, he greeted each one of his lovelies in turn.

He started with Rosie.

She blinked back at him, her beady eyes peering from tangerine orbs through the clear glass separating them. Her smooth, tawny scales gleamed under the bright light warming her house. Rosie was a red-eyed crocodile skink. She'd been hard to find.

Native to New Guinea, Owen had searched the few pet shops that imported exotic breeds, and had finally settled on obtaining her directly himself. The paperwork was a nightmare. But it had all been worth it when Rosie arrived.

She was a fine specimen, rare and beautiful, and fit in nicely with the rest of his collection. He often caught her peering through her glass house into the houses of the others. Owen knew she felt at home here, that she realized she'd been brought into a home of the highest quality, amongst other amazing breeds.

Rosie blinked at him twice in quick succession. He smiled.

Owen moved on, stopping next to check in on Lucifer.

At first glance, Lucifer didn't appear to be in his glass home. Of course, he had to be. All the glass houses were one-hundred-percent secure. Owen checked them three times every day. He'd already made a check earlier before he'd gone to the grocery store.

He peered into the glass tank, looking for Lucifer. Green, iridescent scales shimmered under the warm light in the top corner of the glass home. There he was. Lucifer made an appearance, slithering from behind a rock to greet his owner, and his feeder. His two-pronged tongue flickered from his mouth, saying hello to Owen.

"Hello, Lucifer," Owen greeted back.

Owen spent a few moments enjoying Lucifer, watching his slithering movements. Lucifer's glass-bead eyes never left Owen. His tongue slipped in and out of his thin mouth, talking to Owen.

Owen continued on. His next stop was to check in on Petunia.

Petunia was a dunner morph. A rare type of bearded dragon from the Australian scrublands. He only learned about the prized species as a result of reading an article in his monthly subscription to *Extreme Exotics*. His interest had immediately been grasped. He'd thought about it for three solid days until he had time to look into the species and where to get it. Using his experience on import paperwork from acquiring Rosie, Petunia soon made an appearance, joining his prized collection.

Owen stared at Petunia. Petunia stared at him. Her body was sleek, shiny, and painted in a symmetrical pattern of pineapple-and-cream scales. It calmed him. Her symmetry. Her perfection.

Lost in a hypnotic reverie, the pattern pulling his mind, twisting his thought, Owen lost himself in an alternate reality. The dual path of consciousness took him away. He saw himself opening the top of Petunia's glass house, reaching in, stroking her perfect patterned body, feeling the smoothness of each scale under his fingers. He saw himself lifting her, holding her in his palms, admiring her.

They weren't in the terrarium anymore. They were in the perfect place, the basement, redone, finished and sublime. The house of perfection, the temperature hot, the air moist, the room dark, except for the bright lights warming each individual glass house, for the beings inside to thrive upon.

The other exotic pets waited in their glass houses, in anticipation.

Completely lost in the other-world reverie, this dream of his imagination, he walked over to the operating table—a long, steel-slab bed. He placed

Petunia with care onto the table. She sat still, blinking up at him.

His hand involuntarily reached over to a set of carefully laid out tools. His fingers knew which one to extract, without him looking, without him thinking, without him controlling his hand.

He pulled the silver tool, sharpened to a point, over toward Petunia.

Petunia sat still, blinking up at Owen.

Owen stood still, blinking down at Petunia.

Bing Bong. A loud ring jolted Owen back to reality. He stared down at Petunia, resting calmly in his palms, blinking back at him. The inadequate walls of the temporary terrarium closed them in, with the other exotic pets.

Bing Bong. The ring jolted him again. His phone? The doorbell? He couldn't be sure. It sounded far away. He'd turned them both up to full volume. The walls and the heavy door almost tuned them out.

Owen walked over to Petunia's glass house and placed her gently inside. He closed the top, double checked that it was secure, then walked over to the terrarium door. He checked the lock three times, then walked through his townhouse, toward the front door.

Owen peered through the peep hole, inspecting the source of the intrusion.

A young woman with thick black glasses and straight raven hair stood on the other side of the door, holding a hefty hardcovered book. She reached out her pointer finger and pressed the doorbell, again.

Bing bong.

This time, Owen responded. He glanced in the large mirror hanging over the shiny black table. Wiping his sleeve over his sweat-coated face, he took a deep breath. He turned back to the door and opened it.

He stared down at the petite woman, her amplified, dark eyes peering back at him though thick lenses. "Good afternoon, sir. My name is Brittany, I represent *Scholars Encyclopedias*. I wonder if I could trouble you for five minutes of your time?" Her eyes peered at him like big fish eyes, keen and eager.

Encyclopedias. Owen thought of the full collection lining his bookshelf in the spare room he'd converted into a library. "Encyclopedias?"

"Yes, sir. We offer the full collection of the standard volumes. In addition, we also offer several special collections, for the more well-read clientele." She smiled. The corners of her mouth twitched.

Was she nervous? Was he acting normal enough? Or was it worry over making a sale? "Special collections?"

"Yes, sir."

"Do you carry any specialty volumes pertaining to exotic reptiles?"

"Yes, sir. We have a collection pertaining to exotic species in general. One of the volumes is focused on reptiles."

He needed that volume for his collection. Now.

"I do carry copies of everything, in the van." She turned and pointed to a periwinkle van, parked two houses down. "I could grab a copy of the exotic reptiles volume for you to look at, if you are interested."

He wanted to see it. Could he risk inviting her in? Sweat sprouted over his top lip. "That would be grand."

She nodded and walked toward the van.

OK, Owen. Look at the book. Don't invite her in.

Petunia's eyes explored his mind. Petunia. He needed to save himself for her. He couldn't let himself…no. He couldn't.

Frames from the series of classic horror flicks depicting his own life—*Owen's Demise, Owen's Living Hell, Owen's House of Blood*—flashed through this mind. One at a time.

The potential future played through his mind in a series of frames.

Flash. Petunia, pinned to the steel slab.

Flash. Petunia, her black, beady eyes pleading with him, blood seeping from the pin piercing into her stomach as she lay on her back, flailing.

Flash. Brittany's dark eyes peering at him through her thick glasses.

Flash. The rare volume of the exotic reptile encyclopedia in his hand.

Flash. Blood. More blood.

He slammed the door and locked it. He walked over to the front window of the living room, overlooking the street. Pulling the curtains shut, he plunked down into a chair and rested his head in his hands.

Bing bong. The doorbell rang.

He closed his eyes and buried his face into his palms. Sweat and tears mixed with the heat of his hands against his face.

Bing bong.

He closed his eyes tighter, shutting out the doorbell.

Brittany's dark eyes amplified like the bulbs on a fish head, peering at him from a blood bath.

Save Brittany.

Petunia's eyes pulsed through his mind, like glowing black orbs, beckoning him.

Save Petunia.

His own eyes, staring into the massive mirror in the front hall, pleading with himself.

Save yourself.

The room whirled around him. The ringing of the doorbell swept away in a vacuum in time, echoing eerily through the space into his eardrums. Sweat poured down his face, over his fingers. He raised his head, settled back against the chair, and concentrated on breathing. He counted down from ten.

Ten.

Flash. The frame in the film, showing Petunia pinned to the slab, grew fuzzy.

Nine.

Flash. The frame burst into flames, burning to nothing.

Eight.

Flash. Petunia appeared, on the steel slab, unpinned. Unharmed.

Seven.

Flash. Petunia sat in his palms. In the basement terrarium.

Six.

Flash. Petunia sat in her glass house, looking up at him.

Five.

Flash. Owen stared at the heavy door of the terrarium. All his exotic pets locked away, safely, in their glass homes.

Four.

Flash. A butterfly with ocean wings perched on a dark, wooden table.

Three.

Flash. The ocean wings fluttered. The butterfly lifted.

Two.

Flash. The butterfly flew away.

One.

Flash. Owen stood in the depths of the forest behind the foster home of the woman who collected children as if they were cats. Owen. Alone.

TRIPLE CREME

The triple-creme brie spread like butter over the slice of freshly baked baguette. Owen relished in a bite, the cheese melting in his mouth. He washed it down with a long, luxurious sip of Beaujolais. The fruit flavour melded with the creamy aftertaste of the cheese clinging to his tongue.

The episode had ended when he blacked out. It took almost an hour as the frames in the film of his future increasingly intensified. He'd counted down from ten over and over, taking a deep breath in and out with each count. Imagining the frames of the future he didn't want burning to nothing, the highly flammable cellulose nitrate melting in its deserved hellish death. Recreating the film with the frames he wanted. The frames intensified, his entire brain buzzed, until black nothing took over.

When he came to, the fires had stopped burning and the hellish future had ceased to appear. The sweat pouring over his face and down his back had evaporated, leaving his body sticky and cold. He'd stripped down, ran a hot bubble bath, and soaked away the memories of the episode. Warm and rejuvenated, he'd put on his purple velour robe and matching slippers, shuffled into the kitchen, and made a fancy picnic. For one.

Sitting in his dark room, his viewing room, he'd selected one of his favourite old classics, put the reel on the projector, and pressed play. As he watched one the most famous werewolves of his favourite era hunting fresh, unsuspecting prey through the dark woods, he picnicked on brie, bread, and wine.

Every pore in his body seeped calm. This was his safe place. The downward slope following the peak of the curve. The curve that dictated his state of being. The bottom brought him a sense of ease. As he climbed toward the top, his discomfort increased steadily. At the peak of the curve, his sickness took over. As he rode the peak, his urges surged, he became increasingly uncomfortable, to the point of sheer pain, until he either gave in, or he blacked out.

He used to give in—in Agnes' basement, his makeshift workspace where he would torture the creatures of the forest. Every time he took the breath away from a living thing, relief would wash through him. He would ride down the other side of the curve, his sense of ease increasing until he hit the bottom.

Now, he had learned to *control* his sickness. He wouldn't cave. He refused to give in. As a result, the peak had widened. His urges would last longer, the pain becoming more intense until he succumbed to an episode. An episode meant black nothing, a loss of time. But it didn't mean a loss of life. Following the episode was some sort of bliss. Like now. Enjoying a fancy picnic and watching a classic flick.

He smothered another circle of bread with creamy cheese and popped it into his mouth. A man ran through the woods, pausing to howl at the full moon as his chest rippled with new muscles, popping the buttons on his shirt, thick tufts of hair poking through.

The cheese melted over his tongue and lingered in his mouth. He lifted a silver goblet and took a slow sip of fruit-infused wine. The warm spice lingered on the back of his tongue, sliding down his throat to join the cheese.

Right now, here in this moment, Owen didn't think about the next upward slope toward the next peak. The hot pokers of pain. The next spot of black nothing. He only thought about the high he felt at this moment. One more triumph. He'd ridden through the pain, and no life had been extinguished.

THE PRAYING MANTIS

July 15, 1980

A composite of ten-thousand mini-eyes, formed into two black beads, stared from a green insect face. Staring Owen down. Or inspecting him. He wasn't sure.

Two harlequin insect arms—bent at where elbows would be, were it human—twitched, the feelers on the ends clawing through the musty basement air. The sleek insect body reached down the back of the creature, its tip touching the wooden table. The creature perched on delicate legs, four of them, each bent at the bottom forming a foot. It hovered in its glass case, waiting for Owen's next move.

The Praying Mantis was a magnificent creature. Owen had been wanting to catch one for a long time. At one point, he'd been unsure as to whether or not they lived in the forest behind the house of the woman who collected children. His research had revealed the possibility that they could survive the harsh climate of the Canadian prairies.

He opened an old book he'd stolen from the library, the spine crackling and the pages tearing free. No one would miss an old rotting book about insects, would they?

He found the page he'd earmarked, the one spouting facts about the Praying Mantis. The awe-inspiring creature. The insect of all insects. In his mind.

Running his finger down the yellowing page, he found the part he was looking for. The female Praying Mantis lured in her mate with a cocktail of pheromones. It was a long, deceitful act she put on, convincing him he'd be safe in her insect arms. After mounting him, drinking his love juices, leaving him weak and dry, she'd clamp her jaws down over his head and devour him in a handful of bites. Sexual cannibalism was her specialty.

Owen's insides tingled with delight even though he'd read the passage a million times.

The ability of the female insect to have such control over her…friend? Mate? Partner? Only to turn him into her *prey*. Owen's brain buzzed with fascination.

The page crackled as Owen turned it. A full-length picture of the female glowed under the bright desk lamp. On the opposite page, an anatomically correct sketch mirrored the picture version, complete with lines pointing from terminology to body parts. A count of six abdominal segments, the last one enlarged, indicated a female.

He looked back at the live version perched on his desk, the composite of ten-thousand mini-eyes inspecting him. He glanced at the row of abdominal segments. He was quite sure it matched the sketch in the book. He wouldn't be *absolutely* sure without closer inspection.

He placed the book on the top, left corner of the desk. Pulling a fresh pair of clear gloves from a box on the top, right corner of the desk, he snapped one over each hand. A sterilized set of shiny, silver tools lined the bottom, right corner of the desk. He chose long tweezers, picking them up with his left hand. With his right hand, he raised the glass jar housing his subject.

Before the insect could respond to the wave of cool air, he clamped its long chartreuse body with the tweezers. Thin legs twitched and flailed through the air as Owen lifted the anthropod and placed it down on its back. Insect arms unbent and reached up toward him, the small walking appendages on the ends of where it would have hands, if it were human, scuttled through the air, trying to ground itself.

Once on its back, Owen held it in place with the tweezers over a square of white oak, in the centre of the desk. He picked up a silver pin, pointed at the end and hollow through its centre. A hollow pin pierced into things easier than a solid one, as the guts of the creature would slide through the empty cylinder, rather than provide resistance.

Owen stared at the insect. Its legs flailing, its tibial spines reaching, its antennas moving back and forth. He took a deep breath in, stuck the tip of the pin into the centre of the body, pushed down, and exhaled as the pin slid through. Green guts slid over the top of the hollow opening at the peak of the pin as it reached the back side of the bug body and stuck into the plastic sheet, then into the white oak.

Unlatching the tweezers from the body, he snatched up a bottle of his homemade cleaning concoction, sprayed the tweezers three times, then wiped them with a clean, white cloth. He replaced the tweezers into the lineup of tools, in the correct spot.

He pulled the book toward him, inspecting the anatomical diagram. Looking back at the pinned Praying Mantis, he counted the abdominal segments. Six. The last one in the lineup was larger than the others. It matched.

His prey was indeed nature's perfect predator, the insatiable cannibal, the female Praying Mantis. Tingles exploded from his gut up to his throat. *Yes.*

Triumphant at his success, he'd captured the insect of insects. His most prized trophy to date.

The script he'd play out ran through his head. He'd worked on it. A lot. It was more evolved than the process he'd been using on the other insects, the ones that were framed and lined the walls of his private shelf in the back corner of the basement. The Praying Mantis—the Queen of the Insects, the most talented and deceitful of them all, able to fool her prey and lure it in— now lay pinned to his workbench. This Queen surely deserved a more drawn out, more meticulous process than the other, lesser insects.

It was time. He'd waited so long for this. To capture this creature, and now, the moment was finally here.

Owen's brain buzzed. Energy raced through his neurons, each step vibrating through his thoughts.

Capture.

Pin.

Gut.

Mount.

Clean.

He wanted every appendage in place. Every piece of this special specimen needed to be maintained. He would slit it open, watch it twitch itself to sleep, gut it out, hollow its insides, clean it, then mount it in a perfect pose, like the hunter it was, in a special golden frame. It would be placed above all the other frames on his secret shelf.

Owen's brain zizzed louder, his head twitching with anticipation.

He eased back against the wooden chair, took a few deep breaths, and slowed the palpitations hijacking his heart. Relishing in the excitement, the building high as his sickness was released. He didn't want it to be over. He feared the other side of this peak, the downward slope of the black feeling that sat in his gut like a brick.

He shook off the thought. No. Nothing would ruin this moment.

Focusing on the insect, the hunter, he watched its erratic movements, jerking, twitching, delicate insect appendages flailing. Nothing in sight to latch on to. The bulbous eyes searching for something to ground itself with.

Owen's eyes sizzled, focusing on the desperation of his catch.

A scan of the row of tools revealed the one he needed next. The cylindrical concave, hollowed out to provide a scoop. The perfect shape to clean out the inside of the lean, green body.

Owen licked his lips, picked up the tool, positioned it at the centre of the shiny body, then pushed it in.

Warm sweat popped out of his pores.

Electricity pulsed in his brain.

FRIDAY FRIGHT NIGHT

The subtle click-click of the reel, clamped to the side of the projector as it spun, echoed through the attic-like space on the top floor of the Elm Movie House.

The movie, the selection of the movie house—which meant the selection of Wilfred—had three minutes and forty-three seconds left. The climax, one of the cheesiest of all time, in Owen's opinion, was twenty-eight seconds away. Even though Owen thought this particular flick to be sub-par, of lesser quality than the better classics, he still enjoyed the climax. He loved the height of any movie. That point when everything came together, for happiness or disaster, followed by a downward slope. An ecstatic high, just like the one he experienced before the downward slope of the curve of his own life.

He stared at the screen, waiting for that moment, stealing quick scans of the patrons scattered across the old movie seats in the theatre below, inspecting their body language, waiting for any minute reaction to the horrific climax in all its cheese-coated glory.

The victim—a curly blonde-haired young woman with perky breasts, wearing a tight, white tank top on a cold night—fake-ran through a forest. The trees loomed over her against the night sky. A peek of the moon showed the glowing bulb, full and round, casting the only light over the forest. The girl ran two steps, turned, screamed for a more-than-necessary amount of time, then attempted to run a couple more steps. She repeated this process several times, a dark shadow crawling closer, also pausing for long lengths of time, rearing its head, opening its jaws, a hellish mix of a scream and a howl echoing through the forest.

The same sequence of frames played itself over and over, taking up 3.7 minutes of the 87-minute flick. The ridiculous sequence of events took up five thousand, three hundred and twenty-eight frames of the film. A repetitive, yet necessary, emotional and dramatic end to secure the film's place in it sub-genre of horror fromage.

Owen delighted in the childish glee surging through him as he watched the scenes on repeat, until the final moment came. The creature creating the shadow caught up to the screaming girl. A claw sliced her neck clean open.

Blood poured over her, in extreme amounts, soaking her tight, white tank top, sticking it to her perky breasts. She fell back against the grassy floor of the forest. The moon hovered overhead. The glow intensified. The face of the beast, revealed in its hairy, grotesque form, took over the final frames of the film.

The movie ended. The reel flapped. Owen snapped to attention, raising the lights in the theatre below.

He pulled a microphone toward him, leaning over the wooden desk housing all the equipment required to execute a film viewing, and pushed a button.

He spoke, slow and enunciated, into the voice amplifier. "Ladies and gentlemen, that completes our viewing of *Bloody Beast*. Please enjoy a fifteen-minute intermission where you may purchase refreshments at the concession. Do stick around for our finale. It's a special one tonight, folks. You true horror fans will not want to miss out on this."

He released the button and stood. He went to work on removing the reel from the projector, carefully replacing it into its circular tin home and putting it aside. The packaged film would stay on the desk until the end of Friday Fright Night when Owen would return both of the films to the cold storage room.

He loved this cozy little attic of a film-viewing room. Up here, he was in control. He could command the attention of the crowd below with his announcements over the microphone, a curtain over his voice, over him. The crowd below would sit for hours, watching the films he played for them.

It felt…right.

The people below filed out of the theatre. Most of them teenagers who loved to hang out on a Friday night, under his watch. They knew they could get away with the things their parents wouldn't let them do. He didn't care. They watched his films. They kept him company.

The theatre grew quiet. All movement ceased. He turned his attention to the preparation of the evening's feature. His selection.

He was about to lift the lid off the tin of the feature he had chosen when movement in the theatre below caught his attention.

She was there. The porcelain doll from the other day when he had to work the concession counter with the too-perky Kelly and her bouncing blonde ponytail.

The porcelain doll.

She'd said she would *see him on Friday*. And here she was. Walking across the theatre floor, her heels clicked through the quiet space, echoing up to the film controller's attic. To Owen's attic. Calling to him. Announcing to him that she was here. To see his chosen feature film. Maybe, to see him.

Hot tingles ransacked his insides. Violating him. He didn't want them to stop. He couldn't look away from her as she gracefully made her way across the room, toward the screen. She paused, scanning the empty rows, investigating seat choices. She selected carefully, choosing a spot three rows back from the screen, in the very centre of the row.

The cup holders on either side were empty. The seats were devoid of any jackets claiming the spot for a returning patron. Did she, like himself, prefer to sit alone, without anyone beside her? Did she, like himself, know that the third row back provided the most up-close view without cranking her neck? The hot tingles intensified, yet, in a less violating way.

Was he becoming comfortable with this new feeling?

She sat down in her chosen seat, setting her medium-sized bag of popcorn down on the floor at her feet and her medium-sized cup of coffee in the cup holder to her right. A creature of habit? She seemed more like him with every observation he made. He hadn't seen her during the previous film. She wasn't there. He would have noticed her. Did she come solely for *his* feature?

The hot tingles heightened into blazing pokers, sticking into him as if his insides were flaming logs in a brick fireplace. It should have been uncomfortable. He didn't shy away. His body ached for this new invasion of raw emotion to continue.

Her soft, milky hand reached for the coffee cup, pulling it toward her full, red lips. She sipped the coffee. He watched her every movement. The red imprint of her lipstick left on the plastic cover of the to-go coffee cup. The delicate movement of her silky hands, lifting the cup to her lips, placing it back in the holder. Her hair. Shining, milk-chocolate locks swirling around the soft pink of her sweater clinging to her shoulders. Clinging to her perfectly poised breasts.

Who was he? He didn't know this Owen. The Owen he was familiar with didn't mingle with a human woman.

A glint from the projector light reflected off the tin case of the feature film. Owen snapped back to the attic. What time was it? He glanced at his watch. He still had four and a half minutes until the start of the feature film. He went back to work prepping the film for viewing. He opened the case, retrieved the reel, slid it onto the arm of the projector, clamped it into place, then fed the first frame through. He turned the projector on, let the first five frames pull through the projector, then switched it off. Perfect. Everything was in place.

He looked down below, verifying that she was still there. That he hadn't imagined her.

She was. In the third row from the front, centre seat.

Chatter cluttered the theatre below as the teenage crowd filtered back in, popcorn and chocolate bars in hands, bottles filled with substances they could only consume in hidden places stuffed inside their jackets crested with the logo of the local high school football team.

The porcelain doll turned her head, milk-chocolate locks fluttering across her pink sweater. She scanned the moderately rowdy crowd, raised an eyebrow, then turned back to the screen, continuing to drink her coffee.

She didn't care. More like him with every observation.

His mind took a wild swing, picturing Rosie, Lucifer, and Petunia for a quick moment. He wondered if this mysterious woman who had slithered into his film house had any pets of her own.

A blip escaped from his watch. He tapped the timer off and pulled the microphone back toward his mouth. Pressing the switch, he spoke in his soft, film controller's voice. "Ladies and gentlemen. Welcome back from the intermission. This is Owen, your film controller, bringing to you the feature film of the evening. *Psycho*, the classic version of 1960 by the horror icon, Alfred Hitchcock. Although this concept has been remade countless times throughout horror film history, I have no doubt you will find this particular portrayal the best you have ever seen. Enjoy the film."

As he released the button, she turned her head, scanning the back of the theatre. Her eyes wandered up, finding the small window into his attic. Finding him. He could have sworn she was staring right at him. An involuntary smile hijacked his face. She smiled, like a satisfied cat. Could she see him through the bright light?

He flicked the switch on the projector. The reel turned and the frames moved through, coming to life one by one on the big screen below. As the movie materialized, Owen alternated between watching the horror unfold and stealing glances at the milk-chocolate locks. She fixated on the screen, only touching her bag of buttered popcorn after the opening credits ended and the first scene was well underway.

A psychological masterpiece took place on the big screen. A young man with a tormented relationship with his mother struggled with the contorted view of the world he'd learned through her eyes. When a young, beautiful woman came into his life unexpectedly, his behaviour reflected the inner turmoil he suffered. He acted out in the only way he knew how.

Owen had always loved this film. He identified with the struggling young man, feeling that they were alike. Only Owen had barely tasted the sour scorn of his mother before she abandoned him. He'd been passed through many hands, landing in the home of the woman who collected children like cats.

A steady *clink-clink* pierced the quiet as a bottle rolled across the theatre floor, coming to a halt with a crash underneath the big screen. Pieces of glass shattered across the floor.

Giggles and whispers echoed through the room, weaving up to the viewing attic. The woman continued to eat popcorn, her gaze fixated on the young man on the screen. Not a flinch, or any indication she cared about the raucous behaviour taking place around her.

She was more like him with every observation he made.

The hot tingles ignited inside him again, sending sparks through his arms and up into his brain. Owen leaned toward the opening in the attic, following the beam of light hitting the screen. He watched the young man observing the beautiful woman. She was unaware.

Owen glanced down at her, observing her movements and reactions. He lost himself in the story unfolding before him, on screen, and in the centre seat of the third row below. He didn't notice the escalating sounds of teenage behaviour. The loud laughter at obscene jokes, the crumpling of empty candy bags, the slurping of lips of a mad make-out session. The sound of the last frame flapping against the projector as the wheel spun snapped him from his reverie.

He stopped the projector. He glanced down into the theatre. The woman was walking toward the exit. His heart raced. Would he ever see her again?

She paused and looked up at him.

Her milky hand waved. His face flushed. His hand waved back. Her heels clicked as she walked up the theatre floor and out the exit.

Heaviness sunk from his throat to his stomach. He turned to the reel, finishing the script of the evening, packing and storing his prized films.

TWILA'S ENTRY

Owen closed the door to the film-viewing attic behind him. He locked it, then clicked the ring of keys to his belt. Descending the rickety old stairs with care, he pushed open the door to the main entrance and walked through. The chandelier scattered sparkles over the plush scarlet carpet. The concession was closed. One employee remained, scrubbing the inside of one of the popcorn machines, the heat wafting out as the machine was only half cooled from its last pop. The scrawny teen emerged from the inside of the hot popcorn house and looked over at Owen.

"Hi, Owen. Geez, it's hot in here." He smiled, wiping the back of his arm across his sweaty forehead.

"Brandon. Good to see you're back." *Glad you were sick. If you weren't, I wouldn't have met...*her.

There she was. Standing near the doors at the entrance. The rest of the room was empty. It was only her, poised on the red carpet, the chandelier diamonds scattered over her milk-chocolate locks.

She turned, finding him with her dark eyes. She smiled.

He smiled back. Involuntarily.

Hot pokers seared his insides. It was a good pain. The kind of hurt that resulted from something completely uncomfortable. New. Unknown. Something his gut told him was a good thing; something he wanted even though he was afraid.

Owen knew the pain was a direct result of his fear. Nothing more. He chose to walk toward the burning coals, crossing the red carpet, over to the porcelain doll.

She came to life. "Hello, again."

That full, luscious red smile. The cloud of orange blossom. The silky, milk skin. She was real, wasn't she?

"Hello, again," he responded. "Did you enjoy Friday Fright Night?"

"I did." She looked at her feet, then back at him. "I'll admit. I only came for the feature."

"Oh?"

"Yes. I looked at the listing out front yesterday. I saw the first film was, well, one of those real cheesy flicks. But the feature. A real classic."

The pokers turned friendly. Easing up on the heat. Warming to a comfortable temperature. He felt like a marshmallow, bloating over warm coals, browning, but not burning. "First time seeing this version of Psycho?"

She giggled. "Oh no. But I could watch it a million times and still want to see it again."

More similar with every observation. With every *interaction*. Flames rose over his cheeks. "I feel the same."

"The feature, you chose that one?"

"Yes, I did."

"I knew it." She beamed.

"You did?"

"Yes. The other day, when you said you were an experienced film viewer, and that you chose the Friday Fright Night feature. I had a feeling you had…good taste." She eyed him up and down playfully.

"Well. Seems like we agree on a number of things." He gulped. Could he keep this up? Not burning on the coals, but playing with the heat. Would he, the human Owen marshmallow, bloat to a pleasant place, or explode in white gloop?

"Well, thank you for letting me know about Friday Fright Night." She turned to the door and opened it.

Cold night air plumed through the warm, butter-coated room. She paused, turning back to him. "Would you be interested in a private viewing sometime? I have a small movie room at my place. I have some old classics that might interest you."

The same. They were the same. How could this be? "That would be delightful."

She passed him a small, folded piece of paper. "My number. Call me and we'll make it a date."

He took the paper. She walked through the door. The door swung closed, pushing the cold air over him, cooling the blazing flames licking through him.

He watched her walk away from the movie house, into the night. Her milk-chocolate hair floated around her in the night breeze. Her long, red coat fluttered behind her. She dissolved into the dark.

He turned the note over. Orange blossom escaped from its folds as he opened it up. The clean, white page was scribed in perfect penmanship.

345-9384

Twila
Your own private Friday Fright Night, choose from:
The Birds
Cat People
The Black Cat

She was an advanced classic horror film viewer.

More like him with every observation. More like him with every interaction. More like him.

Just like him.

She was real, wasn't she?

He looked back across the empty room, Brandon still sweating away inside the popcorn maker. He emerged. "Who was that?"

She was real. "Oh. Just a friend."

Brandon winked at him. "Yeah. Sure she was." He grinned and nodded, sweat pouring down his pimply face.

PINNED LILLY

September 14, 1980

The stairs creaked, warning him.

Owen stared down at the little girl lying on the wooden worktable. Her long, ginger hair was fanned around her head. Blood trickled over her fingers and down her arms, seeping from the holes in the centre of her palms where he'd pinned them to the table. Like a butterfly.

Her little hands were like butterfly wings. Their fluttering movements ceased due to the long silver pins piercing them, holding them against the cracked wood.

The footsteps gained speed, creaking in a fast beat toward him.

Mrs. Harden's voice followed, shrill and commanding, "Owen. Are you down here? Have you seen Li—"

Her footsteps and shrieks came to a sudden halt. Silence ensued as she examined one of her collectible children, pinned like an insect.

Owen froze. He stared at Lilly. Her lips trembled, tears streaming down her soiled cheeks. Disbelief seeped from her rust-coloured eyes.

Mrs. Harden—Agnes—finally spoke, her usually commanding voice a mere croak, "Owen. What have you done?" She walked up behind him, leaned over Lilly, and cupped Lilly's cheek in her work-roughened hand. "Lilly. Can you hear me?"

Lilly's rust eyes wandered, a haze clouding her focus. She nodded.

Mrs. Harden's back straightened as she regained some of her composure. "Lilly. You're going to be OK. You just lie still." She turned to Owen. All of the usual sternness, and more, returned to her voice. Her small mouth frowned, wrinkles riddling the corners. "Owen. What have you done?" She wagged her bony pointer finger into his face, spit flying from her mouth. "You go to your room. Don't you even *think* about coming out until I tell you to."

A quiver trickled over Owen, starting with his lips, migrating down his shoulders and walking through his spine, one vertebrae at a time. He looked at Lilly's face. He looked at her hands. There was so much blood.

He turned his own palms up and stared down at them. Blood. So much blood. It was everywhere. What *had* he done? His brain was numb. His insides were heavy. All he knew was that he'd been walking in the forest, searching for another insect friend.

He'd been feeling bad. Real bad. That dark, gloomy feeling that pulled his insides into a knot and weighed down his heart and his gut as if they were giant bricks. It had been getting worse. Each time he found a friend in the forest, brought it to his workshop, and helped it die slowly, he would feel a great sense of relief. Lately, the relief would only last for an instant.

He remembered walking through the forest, wondering what to do. He'd turned back toward the house when he saw Lilly playing on the swing set. All alone.

From that moment on, it was like he was on autopilot. He remembered talking to her, convincing her to come with him and see something really cool down in his workshop.

He remembered telling her to lie on the table and close her eyes or she would ruin the surprise.

He remembered the tingles that shot through him and sent his brain buzzing the moment he pierced her palm with the long pin. Her cries still rang through his ears. Sparks of elation were still setting off in his brain, searing through him like fireworks.

"Owen." Mrs. Harden grabbed his arm with her bony hand, her fingers digging into his wrist. "Did you hear me?"

He didn't know what to do. He nodded, then took one last look at the holes in Lilly's hands and the blood trickling out of them.

He turned and walked to the stairs at the edge of the dark basement, wrapping the image up and storing it in a scrapbook of memories he was building in his mind.

Owen shoved Mrs. Harden from his mind, walked up the creaky stairs, and went into his bedroom. He was glad the other two boys he shared the room with—Roy and Thomas—weren't there. He lay down on the bed, let his head rest back into the pillow, and closed his eyes. His hands sunk into the white sheet, staining it red. He replayed the scene with Lilly over and over in his head, reliving the internal fireworks each time he saw the pin slide into her hand. He wanted to hold on to this feeling. It was the polar opposite of the bad feeling that had its hold on him so much of the time.

He sighed and let the sparks set off inside of him one more time.

PRIVATE FRIGHT NIGHT

The doorbell rang—an eerie tone seeping through the door and into the pits of Owen's ears. The sound clung to the night air, to the space on the other side of the door.

What was he thinking? Was this really a *date*? A storm raged in his gut. Maybe he should leave.

The door swung open. Orange blossom wafted over him. Her full red smile soothed his insides.

"Owen. Come on in."

What was he thinking? Leave? The old Owen was still talking to him. Hijacking his thoughts. As soon as he heard her voice, saw her face, the new Owen was strong and present.

"Thank you." He followed her into the house. Warmth wrapped around the cozy front room. Flames licked the sides of a brick fireplace. A bottle of wine sat on a glass table. Next to it, two wine glasses, a corkscrew with an ornate ivory handle, and a small aerator were positioned in perfect placement on a garnet cloth.

Owen's newfound, involuntary smile took over his face. Warm coals settled into his core, warming him from his gut to his heart.

She closed the door behind them. "Are those for me?" She eyeballed the six red roses he'd carefully selected and had wrapped in a clear paper at the Flower Mart down the block from the movie house.

"Yes." He handed the flowers to her.

She took them, lowered her nose into the lush, red petals, and breathed in deeply. "Wonderful." She led him over to the fire, the wine, the cozy setting. "Please, sit. I'll pop these into some water. Do get comfortable. I thought we could enjoy some wine before the film." She walked toward an adjoining kitchen.

Owen sat on a black leather couch. The surface was soft and supple. He leaned back and ran his hands along the luxurious material. He scanned the room. She had good taste. The rug was creamy and plush. The walls were painted a royal blue. The furniture was a dark wood of fine craftsmanship.

He leaned over and looked at the bottle of wine. It couldn't be. *Monte Real.* A Tempranillo from Rioja.

She emerged from the other room. "I hope you like red. Tempranillo isn't common, but I love it."

"I love it, too."

"You've had it?"

"Yes. This label, in fact. I have three bottles at home."

"Well, then. Our tastes seem to be similar. Horror movies—the classics, of course. Wine. Hmmm, what else?"

"Do you have any pets?"

"I do. I hope that's not a problem."

He shook his head. "No, not at all."

She picked up the bottle of wine and the corkscrew. "Well, I have a soft spot for felines. In fact, here comes one of them now."

A dark-haired cat walked stealthily across the room, eyeballing Owen up and down.

"That's Fifi. She's one of my older ones. Almost twelve now. She's well behaved. She's adapted to…my rules. So, I let her roam." She twisted the opener, now plunged into the cork. She pulled. The cork popped.

Fifi walked up to Owen, brushing against his leg. She purred, pressing against him. His shin vibrated.

"Oh my, she likes you. She doesn't like many people." She settled the aerator over one of the wine glasses and poured. Ruby fingers stretched over the bowl of the glass. Hints of fig and cedar plumed through the room. "Do you have pets?"

"Yes. Not the typical kind."

She raised an eyebrow and lifted the bottle, then handed him the glass of wine. "Oh?"

He took the glass. "Reptiles. Exotic reptiles. Very interesting breeds."

She poured Tempranillo through the aerator into the other wine glass. "Incredible. I always wished I had more interesting pets. But there's something about a cat that I can't get away from."

Owen moved the glass beneath his nose and breathed in. A hint of tomato joined the fig, a touch of tobacco melded with the cedar.

She put the bottle down and moved over to the couch, settling next to Owen. Her dark eyes found his. "Exotic reptiles. Do tell more."

He lowered the glass, waiting for his hostess to lead the indulgence. "It all started with Rosie." He paused. "Well, actually, it started long before that, when I was a teenager." The forest behind Mrs. Harden's house loomed in his mind. He shook it off. "But now, in my current home, it started with Rosie. She's a red-eyed crocodile skink."

"What?"

"Yes. She's from the tropical rainforest in New Guinea. She looks a bit like a gecko."

She stared at him, her dark eyes growing with intrigue. "I would love to hear more about Rosie. But first, let's toast to interesting pets." She leaned her glass toward his.

Their glasses clinked. She raised her glass to her luscious lips, closed her eyes, and took a long sip. Owen stared, mesmerized by the ruby liquid seeping over her scarlet lips. He took a long sip from his own glass. The incredible flavour tickled his senses.

"Please, Owen, tell me more about this Rosie."

Rosie's tangerine-encased black eyes stared into his mind. "Her body is beautiful. Tawny scales, shiny and smooth. She pays a lot of attention to the others in my collection."

Twila nodded, taking another long pull from her wine glass.

"This wine is such a delight. Every time I drink it, it's like the first time," he said as he watched her drink.

"I feel the same way." She paused. "What other exotic creatures do you have?"

Owen flipped through the images of the exotic beings in his catalogue of creatures. "First, you tell me more about Fifi. Do you have other cats?"

"Such a gentleman." She smiled.

Heat blazed through his core.

"I do. I have thirteen. I know, it seems like a lot, but, like you, I like to collect different types. Interesting breeds."

More like him. With every interaction. With every observation.

Owen beckoned the blaze building inside of him. He was ready to walk into the unknown. The interaction with a human woman. This human woman. He took a long sip of Tempranillo and settled back into the couch, listening to the description of thirteen different breeds of feline.

PINEAPPLE AND CREAM

Owen loved Petunia. He loved her so much, in fact, that as he stared at her now, through the glass panes of her house, his insides caved in upon themselves as he struggled with his next move. The pain in his head, in his arms, in his gut, had become so intense he almost couldn't function. He'd called in sick at the Elm Film House this morning. He had never once, in his ten years there, missed a shift.

When his alarm went off that morning, he could barely move his arms and his legs. They were heavy and throbbing. He had manoeuvred his arm of bricks over to the nightstand, picked up the telephone, and dialled the film house. He had explained between thunderous throbs of pain thrashing his entire skull that he could not come in. Due to his impeccable record, Wilfred was extremely understanding.

After three hours of tumultuous thought, spinning his options over in his mind, he'd come to the same conclusion for the thousandth time.

He had to take action. He had to release the urges seeping through him. He didn't know what else to do.

Now, standing here in his purple velour bathrobe and matching slippers, he stared at Petunia and silently wept inside.

Petunia blinked. Her beady eyes stared at him with what he interpreted to be love. If a reptile could love. Regardless, she looked calm, in her comfortable glass house.

He sighed, heavy and deep, then lifted the top of the glass house. Reaching into the warmth of the enclosure, he picked Petunia up and lifted her. She settled quietly into the box he set her in, continuing to blink her beady eyes at him. Owen placed the lid on the box and swallowed against the ball of bile and acid rolling up his throat.

Owen lifted the box, walked across the makeshift terrarium, and exited through the heavy door. It clicked behind him as it secured. He checked the lock three times, then walked down the hallway.

His new terrarium, the one in the basement, wasn't quite ready. It was close enough. It would have to do. He simply couldn't take the pain anymore.

Claws scuttled across the bottom of the cardboard box. Petunia's feet pressed into Owen's palms as she scurried around the floor of the cardboard box. He balanced the box on his left hand and pressed his right hand against the lid, ensuring it didn't pop off.

Owen swallowed. The few drops of saliva in his dry mouth scraped down his throat. He breathed in, filling his stomach with air, holding it, then releasing it in a mini-meditation, a meek attempt to accept Petunia's fate.

He racked his brain for the millionth time, trying to comprehend why he was surging on an upward peak to the climax of pain and discomfort. After a wine and horror film evening at Twila's, the most amazing Fright Night he could ever imagine, he'd returned home to a hot bath and a deep sleep. He should be on a high. But he wasn't. He was on the lowest low he'd ever felt.

It was even worse than the heavy gloom that had weighed him down as he watched Lilly swinging back and forth in the backyard of the woman who collected children. A flash of blood drenching Lilly's hands shot through his mind. A chill trickled down his insides.

He had no choice. It was Petunia or Twila.

Sliding his left thumb over the top of the box, keeping the rest of his fingers on the bottom, he reached out and opened the door to the basement terrarium with his free hand. He stepped onto the first stair. The door clicked behind him. Complete darkness cloaked him. He reached out to where he knew the light switch was and flicked it. Fluorescent lighting buzzed. The terrarium below came to life in a buzzing glow, a bright hue, an artificial lab glowing bright.

Owen made his way down the stairs, his purple slippers slapping the bottoms of his feet. He held the box tightly with both hands, not wanting Petunia to make an unexpected escape.

As he stepped from the last stair onto the shiny, white floor, he scanned the far wall lined with empty glass houses. He hadn't fully tested them yet. It wouldn't matter. Petunia wouldn't be in her new house for long. He picked the one in the centre of the wall, walked up to it, opened the lid to the box, and transferred Petunia into her temporary home. She blinked back at him, hardly perturbed by her journey.

Her perfect pineapple-and-cream scales shone down her back under the bright lights. Each scale exactly sized and positioned to form a symmetrical pattern of the utmost precision. Owen's heart tingled. She was perfect. His brain buzzed, foreshadowing the high he would feel.

He walked over to the steel slab in the centre of the room under a bright light and took inventory on the set of shiny, silver tools laid out on the bottom corner of a matching silver desk to the right of the slab. Each tool was present and in the correct location. Pulling a pair of gloves from the box on the top corner of the desk, he snapped one onto each hand. Sliding a fresh sheet of plastic from a roll, laying it from the top to the bottom of the steel slab, he pulled the end against the sharp silver teeth of the cardboard dispenser.

Everything was ready. It was time. Owen walked back over to Petunia's temporary glass house, picked her up, and set her carefully onto the steel slab in the very centre. She blinked up at him, sitting calmly, waiting. But did she know for what?

Owen reached out and took Petunia's claw in his hand. Her scaly skin tickled his finger; her sharp claw traced over his palm.

Owen looked into Petunia's beady black eyes. He stared for a long moment, losing track of time, losing track of himself.

Did he have to go through with this? A violent throb smashed his skull. Hot pain seared his arms.

Sickness swirled a violent storm in his stomach. His insides wrenched.

Yes, he did. He had no choice.

Owen faced his fate. He stared right into the beady eyes. He plucked a long tool from the desk, lifted Petunia, and placed her on her back. He legs flailed tiny circles in the air to no avail. He held her in place.

His pin-holding hand trembled. He paused. Another throb smashed his skull. Pain singed his arms. A tornado of nausea whirled up his insides.

He gave in.

As he slid the hollowed-out pin into Petunia's stomach, he stared at her beady black eyes. The throbbing eased. The hot pain dulled. The sick storm halted.

Something happened to Petunia. She didn't seem like herself anymore. She morphed in front of him. She became a mere object. A toy.

His mind contorted. All thoughts of his love for Petunia disintegrated.

The throbbing eased to a tiny tapping. The hot pain cooled to a slight chill. The nauseous waves became tiny ripples.

Owen's mind cleared. His focused tuned. He took the next step in the script he had written years ago, before his encounters with the insects in the woods behind Mrs. Harden's house.

The sickness swirling in his stomach settled.

A pulsing warmth replaced it.

The script from all those years ago flashed through his mind, one step at a time.

Capture.

Pin.

Gut.

Mount.

Clean.

He placed imaginary checkmarks beside each step until he reached the next one to execute.

At the very peak of his tortured journey—the high, the place where he felt good and like he was OK—he took a moment to relish it. The elation would heighten. It would be the best moment he'd had in a long time. Then, after, the downward slope would be terrifying. He wouldn't think about that right now.

He stared into the beady black eyes and proceeded with the next step.

MERLOT AND MANCHEGO

Owen held the stem of a wine glass with his pointer, middle finger, and thumb. He swirled it. Luscious, mahogany arms reached up the glass bulb. Black spice and currant floated from the top of the wine glass, drifting across his nose. He leaned the glass toward his face and took a deep breath. His back eased into the plush chair. He brought the wine glass to his lips and savoured a long sip. An ample mouthful of Merlot lingered over his tongue. Sweet berries and hints of wood coated the back of his throat.

He settled in against the chair, his legs stretched out in front of him, his purple-slippered feet resting on the ottoman. The wine glass perched in his hand, the bottom resting against his purple-robed upper leg.

The calm after the storm. The steady, flat line before the downward slope. The place he wished he could be forever, without any of the work it took to get there.

The bad thing was that Petunia would never blink her beady eyes at him again. The good thing was that Petunia was now mounted, the first trophy in his new basement terrarium. He'd be able to look at her anytime he wanted to. Another good thing was that he was in the appropriate state of mind to call Twila and set a date to return her hospitality.

Twila. What was it she'd said when he was at her house? Like him, she liked to collect different breeds. Would she understand his *activities?* It was a foolish thought, for sure. Why did he even entertain the idea for a split second? He couldn't explain it. He shooed the idea from his mind, feeling stupid.

In his state of elation, his mind had gone wild. That was it.

He took another long, luxurious sip of the Merlot. He looked at the bottle, perched on the glass coffee table in front of the fire. A vintage he'd only had once before. He'd been saving this bottle for a special occasion. What could be more special than feeling better than he had since…well…he wasn't sure if he'd ever felt this good.

Owen leaned forward, placed the wine glass on the table next to the bottle, then picked up a slice of the Manchego he'd laid out on a platter. He bit into it. The richness blended well with the spicy aftertaste of the Merlot. He plucked a piece of freshly baked just-sliced baguette from a basket next to the platter and leaned back in the chair.

This might be the most perfect picnic he'd ever had.

It was good luck he'd found the three-year aged Manchego at *Penny's Cheese Market*. Penny usually imported primarily from Switzerland and Holland. Rarely did he see a cut of cheese from Spain. He'd never seen one three years old. It was serendipitous. He knew it would be a perfect match for the bottle of Merlot settled in a slot in his wine rack.

Perfect. Everything was perfect.

Crumbs rolled down his purple robe as he bit into the fresh bread. He brushed them off, swallowed the soft dough, then reached for the wine glass again. After another long sip, he set the glass down and reached for the phone on the table next to the chair.

He picked up the receiver and dialled Twila's number. The numbers had engraved themselves in his memory the moment he read the note she'd slipped him at Friday Fright Night.

The phone rang on the other end. Once. Twice. Three times.

Click. "Hello?" Twila's sweet voice soothed his ears.

"Twila. It's Owen." He smiled.

"How wonderful to hear from you." The warmth seeped from her voice, travelling through the wires and coating him from head to toe.

Tingles ran down his arms. "I'm calling to invite you over to my place. To return your hospitality."

"How lovely."

"How's Thursday? Friday I need to be at the film house."

"Thursday is perfect. What time?"

"How about seven o'clock. We'll have a wine-and-cheese pairing. We can watch a film in my projector room." *What type of wine should I serve? Oh, and cheese, I'll have to get more cheese.* He hoped the market had something special on Thursday. He wanted it fresh.

"You have a projector room?" Excitement trickled from her voice.

"I do."

"How exciting. Seven is fine. I'll see you then."

"See you then." He replaced the receiver with a click, then retrieved his wine glass. He settled back into the chair and pondered the collection of films he had, searching for the perfect one.

Perfect.

Everything was perfect.

WHITE WALLS

October 15, 1980

The white walls glared down at Owen, closing in on him. The bright fluorescent tube lining the ceiling electrified his eyes. The tube buzzed, flickering. It went off. It blinked back on, frying his corneas. He pressed his eyelids together tightly. Multi-coloured shapes swam across his vision.

If only he could get out of here. If only he wasn't tied to the bed.

He pulled his arms up. The tight binds dug into his wrists. Burning pain throbbed across the raw skin. He should lie still, but he couldn't resist testing the binds one more time. They were secure. They wouldn't budge.

Owen sunk back hard into the bed, his sweat-soaked shirt plastered to his chest. Chills shivered down his body. Was it his fault he'd ended up here? Could he have chosen to leave Lilly swinging back and forth in the summer breeze? Could he have resisted the building urges, lived with the increasing pain?

At the time, it seemed as though he had no choice. Like he was a robot, executing commands from the curve of his life that had a strong hold on him.

Now, lying here in this bed, in the institute they'd shipped him to, he wondered if there had been another way. Could he have *chosen?*

Mrs. Harden—Agnes—would never want him back. The look of pure disgust riddling her old face said so. The other kids stared in fright, tears staining their cheeks as they huddled together in the small front room, watching the medics wheel Lilly out of the house on a stretcher.

They thought she would make it. Be all right. Or as all right as she could be after the trauma inflicted upon her. At least this was Owen's understanding, according to the snippets of conversation he'd heard as the medics attended to Lilly while he sat, cuffed and watching from the corner, pretending to listen to the uniformed officer next to him who drilled him with questions.

The fluorescent tube buzzed off again, in perfect time to the three-minute cycle it seemed to be on. Owen had spent hours counting the seconds, fairly sure the cycle was three minutes. He opened his eyes. The dark room soothed the humming in his ears, the buzzing in his brain, the constant vibrations pulsing in the pit of his eye sockets.

He wasn't sure how long he'd have to lie here tied to this bed in the private room of the mental institution. They were all afraid of him. Afraid of what he might do. He could have killed Lilly, they all said. What kind of child kills another child, they all said. Their whispers haunted him as he sat in comatose silence in the wheelchair they'd perched him in, his hands secured to the arms.

Their words seeped into his mind as they wheeled him from room to room, performing test after test, assessing him, investigating his mind. Them. The white-clothed, white-shoed, pale-faced attendants. They all talked about him as if he wasn't there. He'd stopped responding the moment they cuffed him.

The lack of response he provided led them to assume he wasn't present. Well, he was. He heard everything they said.

He got himself into this. He needed to get himself out.

He would stay in this silent state until they finished assessing him. It would allow him enough time to gather all the information he'd need to form the correct sentences to grant him release.

The fluorescent tube blazed on again. His eyes burned. He shut them, welcoming the rainbow of weird shapes floating across his vision. This would be good practice, he supposed, to be here, alone in this room, needing to find a way to calm himself, to focus, to get through this.

He needed to step into another internal state. If he could learn how to do that, perhaps he would get out of here. Perhaps he would be better equipped when—if—he entered the world again. To control his urges. To blend in.

He thought about the questions the officer had thrown at him, and the answers that blinked through his mind like a neon sign.

How did he get Lilly down to the basement?

It was easy. She was easy as pie to influence. Her brain was like silly putty.

Why did he bring her down here?

To examine her. To pin her. To help her find rest.

Where did he get these tools?

Each trip to Henry's Hardware store I slipped one into my pocket.

And this *solution* in the bottles? What is it? How did you get it?

I made it, you moron. It's a simple PBW solution. Household ingredients from Mrs. Harden's stash in the basement closet. Safe, alone. Strong enough to remove any stain, when mixed.

A whoosh of cold air jolted him from his workshop, back to the institution room. The white was driving him crazy. The walls. The stiff uniforms. The shoes. Everything was white.

An attendant walked across the room over to him and peered down. He stared back at her brown eyes.

"Owen. How are you doing?" Her sweet voice sounded fake.

Should he speak? He wasn't sure. He faked a small pout.

"Oh, dear, you must be frightened."

Liar. But, yeah, sure. He frowned deeper.

"Well, I'm going to take off your restraints. I'll help you up, into the wheelchair again." She smiled. "Don't worry, we're finished all the tests. The next part is easy. You'll have a chat with Doctor Brown. He's a nice man. He'll help you."

Hmmm. A doctor, huh? Did he have enough intel to say what was required?

Owen nodded meekly, maintaining the frown.

The attendant smiled wider. A second attendant joined, wheeling a chair into the room. This one had blue eyes. They were twins in stiff white, one brown eyed and one blue eyed. He could play them. Then, he'd figure out how to play the doctor.

INSECT PREY

The final frame of *Cat People* flickered across the white screen. Owen's insides tingled. It had been his first time viewing the horror classic from 1942. He felt it was the perfect concoction of paranoia and thriller, depicting the dilemma of Irena, tempted by an interesting and persistent suitor, yet tormented by the possibility that she could transform into a murderous werecat if aroused.

Twila, the owner of thirteen breeds of feline, had brought her copy over, eager to share it with him.

He stole a glance to his left, scanning Twila's face, anticipating her reaction. Her luscious, scarlet mouth broke out in a wide smile as she nodded her head in approval. Her milk-chocolate locks bounced around her shoulders.

A warmth rose through Owen, from his gut to his heart, and up his throat. She was perfect. Too perfect. An old memory hijacked his brain, flashing like a frame in the horror flick of his own life. The frame of the past revealed the Praying Mantis, pinned to the old wooden desk in Mrs. Harden's basement, his workshop. The bulbous ocellus of the insect, composed of ten-thousand mini-eyes, stared him down.

"I can't believe you've never seen this one," Twila's silky voice wove through his ears. She leaned in closer, a cloud of orange blossom erupting from her pores.

"I can't, either. What a gem." A chill trickled up his spine. The remnants of the film clung to his mind. An uneasiness crept through him.

"Well, better late than never." She smiled. She put her milky hand on his arm.

His skin tingled, warm goosebumps sprouting up his arm and over the back of his neck.

He didn't want her to leave. "How about a nightcap?" Should he show her his terrarium?

"That would be lovely." She licked her top red lip.

"Shall we retire, then, to the sitting room? The fire should still be burning strong. We can have a cocktail, warm ourselves, before the night ends." He reached out his hand to her.

She took his hand in hers, her skin soft and supple against his fingers. He led her from the film-viewing room, up a staircase, and back onto the main level of his townhouse. He praised himself for splitting the basement into two. One half for the film room. The other half for the new terrarium, the final place for his exotic friends. In anticipation of Twila's visit, he'd finished the terrarium in haste, putting on the final touches. He had yet to move his exotic friends to their new home. Only Petunia resided down there in the warm humidity.

He wasn't quite sure why he'd been in a rush. He didn't need to take Twila to the basement to show her his pet collection.

The warmth of the flames welcomed them, flushing Owen's cheeks. He guided Twila to a plush reclining chair right beside the fireplace. "Make yourself comfortable."

"Thank you. I will." She eased into the chair, her hair shining from the blaze of the fireplace.

"Shall I fix you a French Martini?"

"That would be delightful."

"I shall return momentarily." Owen walked toward the kitchen.

He turned to face the counter, opening up onto the living space. He stole glances at Twila curled up in the chair by the fire as he mixed her drink.

"How did you know I liked French Martinis, you sneak?" Her playful tone tickled him.

"You mentioned it, when you hosted movie night."

She raised an eyebrow. "Hmmm. I guess I did. Well, what a lovely surprise. A perfect end to a perfect evening." She narrowed her eyes at him.

The composite of ten-thousand eyes flickered through his mind. He paused, shaking his head. Why did nature's perfect predator keep popping into his mind? He rested his palms on the counter. Unless…was he having urges? No. He couldn't let that happen. It had only been two days since his…*encounter*…with Petunia. He was sure he had plenty of time until the next upward slope.

"Are you all right over there?" Twila's voice jolted the spinning in his mind to a halt.

"Oh yes. I was just…ensuring I had the exact measurements." He smiled at his quick thinking. "I wouldn't want to ruin the perfect end to your perfect evening."

"I appreciate your meticulous manner." Again, her eyes narrowed.

The persistent image of the ten-thousand mini-eyes molded into two black orbs that pierced his mind. He shook his head, forcing the image away. He focused on the cocktail, measuring two parts vodka, one part pineapple juice, and a quarter part Chambord. The silver shaker chilled his hands as he shook it. Sweet pineapple and raspberry wafted over his face as he poured the translucent pink liquid into a chilled martini glass. Putting the final touch—a glossy maraschino—onto the special drink, he delivered it to Twila.

She took it, relished in a sip, then looked at him. "Perfect." She smiled. About to take another sip, she paused. "Aren't you having anything?"

"Oh yes. You enjoy your cocktail. I will have mine whipped up in a flash." He walked back to the kitchen.

Gathering the items for the classic martini, he rinsed out the shaker and went to work. French Martini for Twila, Classic Martini for him. It was more…*manly*…wasn't it? In the insect world, the standard roles of human society didn't apply. The Border Mantis female, for example, was much larger and stronger than the male. In the wild, she was in charge.

He shook his head while shaking his martini. As he poured the potent liquid into a martini glass, matching the one he had handed to Twila, and also chilled, he looked across the room. She was curled into the chair, cradling her pink drink, obviously enjoying the warm blanket the flames wrapped around her.

He picked up his glass, walked over to the sitting room, and sat in a chair across the room, on the other side of the fire from Twila.

"Are you enjoying your drink?" he asked her.

"Yes. It's delightful. You're quite the host. You've spoiled me. The wine, the post-film cocktail…I'm not sure I can drive in this condition." She stretched her legs out over the ottoman, narrowing her eyes at him again.

Was she playing? Was she hinting?

"You are welcome to stay. I mean, for your safety." Is she safe here? The thought poisoned his mood in a single prick. What? Of course she is. Was he trying to *convince* himself?

"That is rather hospitable of you. I may just take you up on that offer."

Hot tingles burst up his body. He hoped she would. He would focus on her, on this…*feeling*…that seemed to hijack his being when she was around. If his roaming thoughts were any indication of an early climb back up the slope, he'd stave them off. He could control himself. He knew he could. If he didn't, then Petunia was for nothing. If he didn't…he might lose Twila.

He gulped. No. That wouldn't happen.

Owen focused on his drink, taking a long sip. The vodka and dry vermouth mix numbed his tongue and burned down his throat. His internals eased into a numbing buzz.

The fire blazed, casting an orange-red hue over the dimly lit room. Twila sipped her drink, a contorted, sensual smile playing on her lips. She twirled a chocolate curl around her finger, staring at him from across the room. Reflections of the flames flickered over her dark eyes.

A composite of a thousand eyes bulged down at him from a crevice in his brain.

Stop it. He scolded his mind. It was only an old memory. Nothing more. A glimmer of the feelings that he once couldn't control. The urges. The desires. The sickness.

He'd come a long way. How many times had he controlled his actions?

He'd do it again. The alternative wasn't an option. He wanted, he *needed* Twila to stay here with him.

"What are you thinking about over there?" Twila's sultry voice seeped across the room.

Owen blushed.

"Oh, my. Are you having *unpure* thoughts?"

Owen smiled.

Twila shot back the final two sips of her drink, placed the glass on the coffee table, on a coaster, then got down on all fours and crawled her way over to his chair, like a human feline. A werecat.

The warm tingles intensified into hot pokers of pleasure, pricking him with sparks of desire.

Yes, he could do this. He *would* do this.

She crawled by the fireplace, the flames glimmering off her shiny, chocolate curls. Her eyes narrowed in a lioness stare as she crawled toward him, her sexual prey.

The female Border Mantis conducted sexual cannibalism. Owen's brain seized. *Stop it. Focus.* He looked at her. He inhaled deeply, forcing control over himself, his thoughts, his movements, his being. All thoughts of insects dissolved from his mind, disintegrating into nothing.

She crawled past the fireplace, reaching the foot of his chair. On hands and knees, she licked her lips, crawling up his legs, into his lap.

"Owen. I want you." Her voice hung in the air, seeping with sexuality.

The hot pokers heightened until the heat was almost too much. He liked it. He didn't want it to stop.

He forced his mind to focus on her and nothing else. Giving in, he let her have her way.

PURPLE SILK

Owen awoke. He stared at the ceiling. The silk sheets soft against his arms, he ran his hands over them. He turned his head, looking out his bedroom window. The moon glowed, bulbous and bright.

Twila was still, except for her chest rising and falling in a deep sleep. Her milk-chocolate locks shimmered under the moonlight piercing through the window. Even in sleep, she looked perfect.

It had been perfect. The entire evening. The beginning, the middle, the end.

He took a deep breath, sinking deeper into the soft bed and fluffy pillow. He didn't feel anything bad. No urge. The only desire within him was the accumulation of hot pokers sparking his neurons.

Twila's chest continued to rise and fall. The moon continued to glow brightly, illuminating the outline of every piece of furniture carefully placed around his master bedroom.

He took another deep breath, exhaling slowly. Had he conquered it? Was Twila the answer?

Should he show her his terrarium? The one on the upper floor where his exotic pets thrived? Or the one in the basement, where creatures entered, but never left?

Would she understand?

His skull wrenched. His shoulders clenched, lifting away from the over-fluffed pillow. A sharp pain pierced his gut. No. It was too soon. He had to tread this new situation with the utmost care.

He took another deep breath as he lay back into the soft feathers.

One step at a time. Maybe, just maybe, he'd show her his pets in the morning.

First, he would ease into this new feeling, this new prolonged ride along an extended peak.

He would sleep through the night, with the answer to his problems by his side.

Twila's breath seeped softly from her lips.

Owen closed his eyes and counted to ten.

He would sleep until morning. He wouldn't make any decisions until then.

HUMAN TERRARIUM

Owen's eyes bolted open. A fluorescent tube glared down at him, electrifying his eyeballs with such intensity, it felt as though his retinas were sizzling.

Where was he?

He blinked hard, several times. The bright bulb blazed into his corneas, frying them. He swallowed hard.

Owen tried to move his arms. He tried to shuffle his legs. Pins pricked down his shins. His limbs were heavy, and they wouldn't respond to the neurons firing from his brain, telling them to move.

He felt…paralyzed.

His frozen limbs sank solidly against a hard, cold surface. He tried again to move his arms, but they were bolted in place. He tried to move his legs, but to no avail. He raised his head and looked down his body. A cold, hard steel slab had replaced his soft, silk sheets. His arms and legs were tied down. No, they weren't. It was his hands…something was pinning them in place.

He pulled at his right hand, willing it to move. Pain seared through him, up his arm, and over his skull.

He raised his head again, finding his right hand with his burning eyes.

His throat tightened as he gulped in air. Blinking several times, an image formed, his senses captured it and sent it along his neural network up to his brain. His mind contorted over the received image.

A long, silver pin-like tool protruded from his hand. Blood trickled around the gaping hole where the pin had entered, pooling underneath his palm, where the pin had struck its end.

What the living hell?

Was this a dream? Had he watched one too many horror films? Was his mind playing with him? Replaying its own scene, its own conglomeration of frames cut and pasted from the thousands of flicks he'd consumed?

Cranking his neck, he looked at his left hand. An identical shiny, silver pin slid into his left hand, all the way through and to the other side. Dark-red syrup oozed over his hand, sticking to his fingers, pooling in his palm.

A burst of cold shot through him. He swallowed. He twisted his neck, moving his head to the right, willing his suspicions to be violently wrong.

There she was.

Petunia. Pinned to a square cut of white oak. Displayed in a perfect pose. The ornate, golden frame he'd chosen bordering her wooden mount.

He was in his own terrarium. The culmination of months of hard work with his own hands, to build the ultimate place for his exotic friends. His only friends. He wanted somewhere for them to live in luxury. He wanted somewhere to house them should he have to make choices to stamp out his sickness when it surged.

His exotic reptile terrarium had been turned into a human terrarium. And he was the first guest.

Acid churned through his stomach and roiled up his throat.

The realization trickled over him, seeping into his pores, seething through his veins. He *was* the Praying Mantis. The male.

He reviewed the frames of the evening as the story of *Owen's Terrible Demise* came to life.

The wine by the fire. The perfect pairing of Provence Rosé and Havarti. The viewing of *Cat People*. The late-night cocktail.

Twila. Curled up by the fire like a cat.

The entire time *she'd* been watching *him*. Inspecting him. With her human ocellus, composed of ten-thousand eyes.

Twila. Crawling across the carpet like a werecat.

Orange blossom saturated the moist air molecules of the human terrarium. Owen lay still. Waiting. For his hunter.

He could feel her approaching. Pinned to the table, helpless in his role as prey, he closed his lips and forced his eyes to stay open against the blazing light. Cold steel chilled his neck.

Her dark eyes hovered over him. His mind wove them into ten-thousand blinking orbs. Orange blossom seeped from her pheromonic pores, drowning him in a thick hunter's perfume.

His mind shot him back to the institution of white walls and white-clad attendants. The place where he'd learned what to say to twist life into the path he desired.

He spread his lips into a full, sickly grin, finding her dark eyes with his own burning orbs. His voice sultry and soothing, he said, "Twila, my love. Enjoy every last bite."

ACKNOWLEDGEMENTS

The writing of every book is a journey with highs and lows. This book would not have flourished into existence without the love and support of family, friends, and fellow authors. Thank you to everyone who inspired me, encouraged me, and supported me along the way.

Daniel Willcocks – Thank you for always seeing what I am capable of, and making me see it too. When I crushed a novella halfway through your bootcamp, thank you for saying, "you should write another one, then."

Taija Morgan – Thank you for loving Owen, for pointing out where things needed to be smoothed over in his story, and for waving your magic editing wand (with a lot of blood and sweat, and maybe tears), to help me make this beloved story of mine the best it can be.

AUTHOR BIO

Julie Hiner spent endless hours during her childhood lost in the pages of books. The only thing that took precedence over a book was her Walkman. To this day, Julie is a hardcore 80s rocker at heart.

After securing a solid education in computer science at the University of Calgary, Julie spent over a decade working on large scale network systems. On a break between contracts, Julie followed her longing to finish a book she had started, a work of non-fiction portraying her personal story of facing fear and anxiety on a bicycle in the European mountains. After some deep soul searching, she decided to write a novel.

Following her fascination of the dark mind of the serial killer, and finding inspiration at a talk given by a local homicide detective, Julie surged down her new path to writing a dark, serial killer novel. She now writes dark crime and horror. She loves detailed research, creating in depth character, and unleashing her inner artist on photos to create the cover and marketing material.

AUTHOR NEWSLETTER

Stay in touch, join my devilishly delicious newsletter.

- FREE e-book – a taste of the 80s Metal Murder series

- True crime snippets

- Horror fun (movies, books, creepy readings and more)

- 80s Metal (sprinkled with rock and metal of all decades)

- Free dark reads and access to book sales

- Early notification of new releases

KillersAndDemons.com

AUTHOR REPERTOIRE

S

Final Track

Det. Mahoney I

80s Metal Murder

KillersAndDemons.com

Acid Track

Det. Mahoney II

70s Acid Kill

KillersAndDemons.com

Soil Solo

Det. Mahoney Novella

KillersAndDemons.com

The Omens Call

Horror Anthology

Edited by Hiner and Willcocks

Featuring 'Room Thirteen' by Julie Hiner

DevilsRockPublishing.com

'Hallowed Killer', featured in Pulp Harvest

BloodRitesHorror.com

'Corpse Forest', featured in The Other Side: Horror

Anthology DevilsRockPublishing.com

'Tuny', featured in Terrace VI: Forbidden Fruit

TheSeventhTerrace.com

If you enjoyed Owen's Terrarium, please consider leaving a review Goodreads(.com), or Bookbub(.com), or your retailer of choice. A review is worth a lot to an author.

Come visit @ KillersAndDemons.com

CPSIA information can be obtained
at www.ICGtesting.com
Printed in the USA
LVHW050242071021
699761LV00004B/77